Se Llama Cristina

Octavio Solis

SAMUEL FRENCH

FOUNDED 1830

SAMUELFRENCH.COM
SAMUELFRENCH-LONDON.CO.UK

SE LLAMA CRISTINA was originally commissioned and developed by the Denver Center Theatre Company, A division of the Denver Center for the Performing Arts Kent Thompson, Artistic Director

SE LLAMA CRISTINA was developed in Hartford Stage's 2012 Brand:NEW festival.

SE LLAMA CRISTINA was part of a National New Play Network Rolling World Premiere with productions at Magic Theatre in San Francisco, CA; Kitchen Dog Theater in Dallas, TX; and The Theatre @ Boston Court in Pasadena, CA.

The production at Magic Theatre opened on January 23, 2013 in San Francisco, California. It was directed by Loretta Greco, with sets by Andrew Boyce, costumes by Alex Jaeger, lighting by Burke Brown, sound by Sara Huddleston, fight direction by Dave Maier, and dramaturgy by Dori Jacob. The Stage Manager was Julie Haber. The cast was as follows:

MAN (MIKE, MIGUEL, MIKI) . . . . Sean San José
WOMAN (VESPA, VESTA, VERA) . . . . Sarah Nina Hayon
ABEL, ABE (SHADOW) . . . . Rod Gnapp
GIRL . . . . Karina Gutiérrez

The production at the Kitchen Dog Theater opened on May 27, 2013 in Dallas, Texas. It was directed by Christina Vela, with sets by Claire Floyd Davis, lighting by Aaron Johansen, and sound by John M. Flores and Veronika Vorel. The cast was as follows:

MAN (MIKE, MIGUEL, MIKI) . . . . .Israel López
WOMAN (VESPA, VESTA, VERA) .Vanessa DeSilvio
ABEL, ABE (SHADOW) . . . . .Jeremy Schwartz
GIRL . . . . Samantha Rios

The production at The Theatre @ Boston Court opened on January 31, 2014 in Pasadena, California. It was directed by Robert Castro, with sets by Gronk, lights by Ben Zamora, music by John Zalewski, and sound by John Zalewske and Veronika Vorel. The cast was as follows:

MAN (MIKE, MIGUEL, MIKI) . . . . .Justin Huen
WOMAN (VESPA, VESTA, VERA) .Paula Christensen
ABEL, ABE (SHADOW) . . . . Christian Rummel
GIRL . . . . Amielynn Abellera

CHARACTERS

MAN (MIKE, MIGUEL, MIKI) – A man in his early 30s of Mexican descent
WOMAN (VESPA, VESTA, VERA) – A woman, early 30s, Mexican descent
ABEL, ABE (SHADOW) – A telephone man in his late 40s
GIRL – A girl in her late teens of Mexican descent

SETTING

All the action takes place in a single bare room of a dingy apartment.
A window upstage. A door on the left. And a doorway on the right.
This space becomes other past apartments.

TIME

Time could be in the late '80s, early '90s. But it's a tricky thing.

(A big white room in an upstairs apartment. Strangely barren, almost robbed of furnishings. There are shadows of objects cast all over the floor and walls, but where are the objects? It's pretty weird.)

*(A window with no curtains. A door on one side, bolted and latched with a chain. A doorway to the other leading off. A table with two chairs facing each other. In these chairs a **MAN** and a **WOMAN** in their early thirties, passed out. Both of them look beat, banged, and bruised from the inside. On the table are half empty bottles of booze, dented beer cans and works for hitting veins: cotton swabs, spoon, a tiny baggie with a stash of dope, a couple of needles and a lighter. There's also a pencil and legal pad with balled up wads of paper on the floor around the table.)*

*(Maybe there's a couch. Yes, a couch with ugly misshapen cushions. There's a phone somewhere. The cradle is on the floor by the couch, but the receiver is missing. And there is a crib too, with pink accents for a **GIRL**. The slats have a blanket draped over them, so you can't immediately see in except up close.)*

*(The **MAN** stirs. A slow procession toward the light. He wipes the slobber from his chin and squints around like he doesn't know where he is. Neither the things on the table nor the **WOMAN** quietly snoring across him look remotely familiar. The **MAN** half-heartedly kicks her from under the table. The **WOMAN** mumbles in her stupor.)*

WOMAN. So…sowhatwesayingabsolutelynokid…

MAN. Hey.
    Hey.
    HEY!

> *(He slams the table in accordance with this final
> 'hey.' The* **WOMAN** *wakes with a wicked start.)*

WOMAN. Fuck.

MAN. Rise an' shine.

WOMAN. What are you lookin' at?

MAN. Nothin'.

WOMAN. What's all this shit?

MAN. I was going to ask you.

WOMAN. Me? How the fuck would I know?

MAN. It's yours, inn't it? Clearly, somebody's been *infusing* some kinda street chemical.

WOMAN. Oh yeah?

MAN. Yeah.

WOMAN. Then what you got dangling there, bitch, a mosquito?

> *(He looks down and is appalled to see a needle
> sticking out of his arm.)*

MAN. AWW! What The Fuuck!

WOMAN. Clearly, somebody is infused.

> *(He plucks it out of his arm.)*

MAN. Ow!

WOMAN. I gotta go home.

> *(She tries to get up but her legs are cottage cheese.)*

Oh Man oh Man oh Man. My legs are cottage cheese.

MAN. I don't shoot up. I never shoot up. I fucken hate the sight of fucken needles.

WOMAN. Where's my stuff?

MAN. Excuse me. Lady. Are these your works?

WOMAN. Hell no.

MAN. Who are you? Do I know you? Do I know your name? I mean, I see… I see the shape of your face, that smudge of woe in your eyes, eyes that keep catching grief and trouble wherever they land, but I can't come up with a title for you.

WOMAN. What the fuck are you talking about?

MAN. Hell if I know.

WOMAN. For your information, holmes, my name is. Vespa.

MAN. Vespa?

VESPA. No. Wait. That's not it. It's. Hold on. Shit.

MAN. Vespa is a scooter.

VESPA. I know that! Shit, it's…it's…

MAN. Wait a minute. What's my name? I don't remember my name.

VESPA. That's ridiculous.

MAN. Then what's my name? What's your name? C'mon, Scooter. What is my name?

VESPA. If you don't know your own name, I sure as hell can't help you. And don't call me Scooter.

MAN. What's with all this paper? And What's That?

VESPA. What, that? That happens to be a crib.

MAN. Is it yours? What I mean is, is that your baby?

VESPA. Hello. Do I look like I got a kid?

> *(With an effort, **VESPA** gets up and goes to the crib. slowly. Slower than that. The **MAN** starts putting all the works in a paper bag on the floor nearby.)*

MAN. What am I doin' here? What time is it? What town are we in? What the fuck is going on!

> *(After some effort **VESPA** arrives at the crib and peers inside.)*

VESPA. Jesus H!

MAN. What's wrong? Huh? What's wrong? Yo. Say something!

(VESPA delicately extracts from the swaddling a fairly tasty-looking leg of fried chicken.)

MAN. What the fuck is that!

VESPA. Seems to be a leg of chicken.

MAN. What's it doing in there?

VESPA. How the hell should I know! That's all there is.

MAN. You mean there's no baby?

VESPA. See for yourself.

(The MAN staggers to the crib to inspect the chicken as VESPA heads for the other rooms.)

Hey! Anyone here? Hello!

MAN. It ain't the Colonel.

VESPA. *(off)* What's going on around here? Hello fuckers!

MAN. Not Popeye's neither.

VESPA. Okay, ha ha, very funny, you can come out now!

MAN. Smells homemade.

(She returns.)

VESPA. Looks like it's you an' me, holmes.

MAN. *(tossing the leg back in the crib)* What would a drumstick be doin' in a baby's crib?

VESPA. Fuck if I know.

MAN. Where you going, Scooter?

VESPA. I told you, quit calling me Scooter.

(VESPA goes for the door, undoes the chain and unbolts the lock, but it won't open.)

The door won't open.

MAN. You sure?

VESPA. You try.

(The MAN tries to open the door but he can't budge it.)

MAN. What the fuck.

VESPA. The window.

(They both try the window but it too remains sealed.)

VESPA. How the hell are we supposed to get outta here?

MAN. It looks like dusk outside.

Or maybe early morning.

That non-committal zone of in-between light.

VESPA. Are you hitting on me?

MAN. What?

VESPA. I'm getting outa here.

(She rushes back to the door and bangs on it.)

Hey! Hey! Open this door! We're trapped in here! Hey, you hear me! OPEN THE FUCKEN DOOR!

MAN. Will you shut up? You're giving me a headache!

VESPA. Anybody! Lemme outa here! Please! Please let me out! Please, Jesus God!

*(**VESPA** starts to cry.)*

MAN. C'mon.

Stop that.

Lissen. Vespa. For what it's worth, my senses tell me that maybe, just maybe, we're still trippin'. You and me and the leg of chicken. Which I don't know what it's doin' in a baby's crib. My senses tell me that something crazy happened in the middle of our dope nod which we can't fuckin' seem to recollect, but which sure as hell is going to come back to us real soon.

WOMAN. My name is not Vespa. I don't know my own name. I don't fucken know a damn thing!

MAN. Okay. Okay. Calm down.

WOMAN. Don't touch me!

MAN. Okay, okay!

WOMAN. Back off! Fuck, I don't even know you! This is your fault!

MAN. My fault! How is it my fault!

WOMAN. I don't know! Maybe it's you who put that shit in my system.

MAN. I swear to you on my gramma's grave, I don't do this. Not ever.

WOMAN. But we did! We obviously did! So explain that.

MAN. Look, I'm clutching at straws here, but I think once this shit wears off, everything will fall into place. We just gotta be patient.

WOMAN. Hold on.

> (*The* **WOMAN** *grabs one of the balled up papers and tries to read its contents. The* **MAN** *follows suit.*)

MAN. I can't make it out. It's in Spanish.

WOMAN. It's like poetry or something –

> (*The phone rings. But where is it ringing from? maybe the ugly couch. The* **MAN** *goes and looks under a blanket. The ringing gets louder, more insistent. The gaps between rings shorten. He frantically dredges the couch for the phone, falling into the mess of cushions. Finally, he locates it and clicks the answer button. Lights change. Sudden nightfall. An opaque glow around the couch as if from some lamp, though there is no lamp. The* **MAN** *is sleepy and drunk.*)

MAN. Ma?

> (*The* **WOMAN** *paces in the shadows behind him as a darkened silhouette. Is that a phone receiver she has? Or a shoe? Something.*)

Ama, is that you?

> (*She stops in her tracks. She sighs. He hears that.*)

I can hear you. You sighed.

> (*She stops again. Speaks in a low shattered voice.*)

WOMAN. I need help.

MAN. Help?

WOMAN. There's no one to call. So I called you.

MAN. Who is this?

WOMAN. Nobody special. Just another ruined heart in the desert.

Hello?

MAN. I'm right here.

WOMAN. You got no idea how alone I am.

MAN. I probably do.

WOMAN. You got no idea the things I been put through.

MAN. Go on.

WOMAN. Shit that would kill a horse.

MAN. Damn.

WOMAN. Shit that would kill an army.

MAN. I hear you.

WOMAN. I been through some trials, lord.

MAN. Okay. It's okay.

WOMAN. I should be dead. I should be in the morgue by now.

MAN. That makes two of us.

WOMAN. I am so fucken drunk and scared and if I don't tell you who I am, there might not be much of me left in the morning.

MAN. Then tell me while there's still enough of you left.

I heard you sigh and in that sigh was someone who grew up good and threw all her faith and love and promise into the men she met and some shit took advantage of that and left her with nothing but 2 a.m. and a little booze and recrimination. And the booze is all backwash and she's gotta fill her mouth with something. And if it won't be razor blades, hell, maybe a little conversation.

WOMAN. You heard all that?

MAN. So tell me your name.

WOMAN. I'm in my house, my big ugly house, all by myself. Drinking. Crying. I sit up in bed and I see headlights streak by the window. I get up and the air is rearranged, different, like there's someone in my kitchen. I think I smell him. I think I hear him picking through the food in the fridge, drinking my milk from the carton.

> *(The shadow of a stranger stretches out from the doorway across the walls behind them, a milk carton in his hands.)*

SHADOW OF ABEL. Three jacks…

MAN. Shit me.

WOMAN. He's home. Mad as hell, something about a card game.

SHADOW OF ABEL. …bum hands all night…

WOMAN. I know his habits. I know his tender side.

SHADOW OF ABEL. and then I get three jacks…

WOMAN. But I'm real acquainted with his mean side.

SHADOW OF ABEL. And still lose.

> *(The **SHADOW OF ABEL** throws the jug of milk across the room.)*

MAN. Then what happens?

SHADOW OF ABEL. What are you lookin' at?

WOMAN. He remembers my refusal. How I won't give him what he wants.

SHADOW OF ABEL. I sure hope you're in the mood, baby.

MAN. What he do?

WOMAN. What every shit-kicker since high school's done to me.

SHADOW OF ABEL. Let's see if we can finally make us a family.

WOMAN. He flushes my birth control down the toilet and then does me, does me rough front and back till he's had enough, then he smashes me in the mouth while he's singing that damn song…

SHADOW OF ABEL. "take it easy, take it easy, don't let the sound of my own voice drive you crazy"…

(*The* **SHADOW OF ABEL** *retreats and vanishes,
singing softly as he goes.*)

WOMAN. but it does, it does, oh yes, it does.

MAN. Okay…

WOMAN. All I ever wanted was to be a teacher, and teach
little ones,
but how can I go to an interview with a shiner? How?

MAN. Go on.

WOMAN. I think I'm dead but wake up in my bed with this
stillness all around. So quiet. Like he mighta killed the
house too. I look around for him, but he's not here.

MAN. Where is he?

WOMAN. He mighta stepped out for some sixes. That's a
drive to whole 'nother county. Ow.

MAN. What.

WOMAN. He knocked four of my teeth out, maybe five.

MAN. Fucker. Is he coming back?

WOMAN. He's bound to. He's my husband.

MAN. Oh shit.

WOMAN. You said it.

MAN. Your old man.

WOMAN. His ring on my finger. Abel.

MAN. That complicates the situation but not so much.
Listen. I know those shitheads. I know shitheads like
him real well.

WOMAN. How?

MAN. I'm one.

WOMAN. What do you mean?

MAN. I had a lady once.
And she got herself pregnant.
And I told her to do something about it
Or I'd leave her.
And she did.
And I left her anyway.

WOMAN. Shit.

MAN. I did her something bad. But we should've known better. I'm paying for it with my life.

WOMAN. How?

MAN. I've exiled myself from the Isle of Pussy. It's been years now. I'm tryin' to atone, really I am.

WOMAN. That means you're not so bad, holmes. You're tryin'.

MAN. Thanks.

WOMAN. So what do I do?

MAN. Got whiskey?

WOMAN. Dewar's White Label.

MAN. Damn, woman. That's my poison. Pour yourself a shotta that.

(She takes the bottle while he pours himself a shot.)

WOMAN. Okay.

MAN. You got it poured?

WOMAN. Yep.

MAN. Snort.

(They drink. She downs a huge portion of whiskey from her bottle.)

WOMAN. Okay.

MAN. Now repeat after me. Dear Abel.

WOMAN. Dear Abel.

MAN. My old man.

WOMAN. My old man.

MAN. You are the dumbest motherfucker on earth.

WOMAN. What?

MAN. Repeat!

WOMAN. You are the dumbest motherfucker on earth

MAN. You just blew your last chance at happiness

WOMAN. You just blew your last chance at happiness

MAN. With the most babalicious of beauties

WOMAN. With the most babalicious of beauties

MAN. The pin up girl of your wet dreams

WOMAN. The pin up girl of your wet dreams

MAN. Now channeling all her Amazonian powers

WOMAN. Now channeling all her Amazonian powers

MAN. To curse the ground you walk on

WOMAN. Curse the ground you walk

MAN. And set upon my house

WOMAN. Set on my house

MAN. A force-field of unimaginable juju

WOMAN. Force-field of blahblahblah juju

MAN. Which if in your malice you dare to cross

WOMAN. Malice you dare cross

MAN. Will burn your dick off and wither your nuts to paste!

WOMAN. Burn your dick off and wither your nuts to paste!

MAN. So stay the fuck away, evil domestic a-hole beater of wives!

WOMAN. STAY THE FUCK AWAY, EVIL MOTHERFUCKER YOU WON'T HAVE MY BABIES NAMED AFTER YOUR FAT BITCH MOTHER AND YOU ARE NOTHING TO ME NOW NOTHING BUT ASHES, A PILLAR OF SALT ON MY TONGUE AND I SPIT YOU OUT NOW AND FOREVER, GODDAMN ABEL!

(Pause while they catch their breaths.)

MAN. Hello?

WOMAN. Man, that felt good.

MAN. Awright. You're safe. Don't look back. Have another shot on me.

(She downs another snort.)

WOMAN. I gotta question.

MAN. Shoot.

WOMAN. What kinda rape hotline is this, anyway?

MAN. Rape hot –, rape, what?

WOMAN. Oh shit. Did I misdial? Tell me you're a counselor.

MIKE. I'm just Mike in Canyon, Texas. I was tryin' to write a poem for my gramma who died tonight in El Paso. You called and saved me from doing it.

WOMAN. So much for that horseshit. Damn, I can't do nothin' right!

MIKE. Look, I did you some good, didn't I? didn't I?

WOMAN. I'm in real trouble. I can't stay in this house. I need me some shelter.

MIKE. I got shelter.

WOMAN. You? You got shelter?

MIKE. I got loads of shelter.

WOMAN. Why should I go with you? One moderately good reason.

MIKE. 'Cause a man in his most lonesome suit of clothes craves nothing but to be there for a woman who needs him. It's no accident you called me. You need someone and I need someone and if all we got in common tonight is a bottle of Dewar's White Label, that's good enough for me.

WOMAN. So you're in town.

MIKE. I live out by the Bucket.

WOMAN. The KFC?

MIKE. House right behind.

WOMAN. That is your idea of shelter?

MIKE. I got a spare bedroom with a bed. I got a blender for margaritas.
TV with a fair number of channels.
And if you wanna be a teacher,
I'll see that you get another interview.

WOMAN. I dunno. What's your name again?

MIKE. Mike. But my friends call me Mike. I write for the local music rag. What's yours?

WOMAN. Fuck.

MIKE. C'mon.
Tell me your name.

VESTA. Vesta.

MIKE. Vesta?

VESTA. As in the goddess Vesta.

MIKE. The Vesta of Highway 87.

VESTA. The Vesta of the Saddleback Lounge.
  I'm a dancer.
  Exotic Dancer.
  Vesta's my stage name.

MIKE. Tell me where you live. I'll be there in ten minutes.

VESTA. No, Mike.

MIKE. No?

VESTA. Be here in five.

> (*She drops her "receiver" and faces* **MIKE**. *Tense standoff.*)

  You're Mexican.

MIKE. So are you.

VESTA. I won't hold it against you.

MIKE. Please do.

> (*They slowly step toward each other.*)

VESTA. Just like that, I'm out of his house

MIKE. Just like that, a real woman's in mine

VESTA. In the shadow of the Bucket

MIKE. Where you keep yourself hid

VESTA. Takin' time to heal

MIKE. While I churn out sucky band reviews

VESTA. I water your Ficus

MIKE. I get you a dentist

VESTA. Who gives me new teeth

MIKE. Smiling for the first time

VESTA. I let you shake my tree

MIKE. That poor little squeaky bed

VESTA. Welcome back to the Isle of Pussy

MIKE. Mercy mercy me.

(Passionate kiss ensues. Lights change back.
VESTA *puts the brakes on the messy romancing.)*

VESTA. Whoa.

Whoa whoa whoa whoa.

You and me.

MIKE. Funny, ain't it?

VESTA. You and me were *involved.*

MIKE. Probably still are.

VESTA. Judas priest.

I don't date Mexicans.

MIKE. Neither do I. Much less exotic dancers named Vesta.
So what's your real name?

VESTA. I don't know. Don't you?

MIKE. All I remember is Sweet lips of Vesta. That was the
title.

VESTA. Title of what?

MIKE. I'm not sure.

VESTA. Bet it's a poem.

You said you were writing a poem for your gramma –

MIKE. No, man. I lost the touch for that shit long ago.

I haven't been able to put down one truthful word
since...

I do music reviews for a local hippy-cowboy rag, that's
all.

VESTA. Fair enough.

MIKE. Did you really work at the Saddleback?

VESTA. This twenty-four-year-old drywaller I was seeing
when I was seventeen liked to watch the girls dance at
the club. He said if I lied about my age, I could try out
and maybe earn some cash. So I did. I love dancing. It's
like my one great disappearing act. Pissed my Daddy
off, though. He's the minister at our church. Calvary
Baptist. Had a Bible verse for every little thing. He tried
to keep me and my sister Marie safe from the evils of

the world. Shit, if everything's bad, how can anything be good?

I had to learn it for myself.

MIKE. Is that why you took up with me? 'Cause I told you I was bad?

VESTA. You're not so bad. Just…badly.

Why did you take me in?

MIKE. You were my last chance to square things with the gender.

VESTA. Was I really your first *Mejicana?*

MIKE. Ever.

VESTA. How was I?

MIKE. Not so bad. Come to think of it, you were kinda insatiable. How was I?

VESTA. Sweet. You cried.

MIKE. It was the kind of love that cripples a man for life. The kind of love that drllls a hole in you just to fill it.

VESTA. That's beautiful.

MIKE. I musta read it somewhere.

(VESTA turns toward the crib.)

VESTA. "My dove, my undefiled, is but one.

She is the only one of her mother.

She is the choice one."

MIKE. What is that from?

VESTA. The Song of Songs.

My Daddy used to recite it from memory to help me sleep.

MIKE. Still a drumstick?

(She looks in to see if the baby is there. She picks up the chicken leg.)

VESTA. Just as well. I always wanted a kid, but dreaded being a mother. I couldn't see having a kid with that brute.

MIKE. You're still wearing his ring.

VESTA. It might could be yours. Wouldn't that piss off dear old Abel.

MIKE. Abel.

> *(**ABEL'S VOICE** resonates all around them in a huge roar.)*

ABEL'S VOICE. BAAAAAAABY! YOU CAN'T RUN FROM ME!

> *(Lights change.)*

MIKE. Leaving town, packing a car, peeling out in a hurry.

VERA. I remember three speeding tickets in two states.

MIKE. Country music on the static.

VESTA. Warm beer and cracker jacks.

MIKE. Drivin' like outlaws, taking any road that leans to the west

VESTA. Little towns with little town names

MIKE. On the long road

VESTA. Until this one night

MIKE. I see you sleeping while I drive

VESTA. My dress hiked up cuz it's too damned hot

MIKE. And your head is leanin' against the window and the passing cars light up your face like a Hollywood starlet. Famous, then not. Famous, then not.

VESTA. I'm dreaming of teeth. My teeth sinking into the kitchen floor like seeds. I see them taking root and these stems come up and blossom into these pretty black-eye daisies. And bees all around.

MIKE. I see your brow knit with trouble, trouble marring the automotive beauty of your interstate face

VESTA. Thousands of bees in my kitchen

MIKE. I wanna make it right. And a voice inside me says make it right

VESTA. Bees wanna swarm inside me

MIKE. A voice I have not heard in all my life

VESTA. So I part my legs and let 'em

MIKE. An invisible hand takes my hand and puts it on the open range of your inner thigh

VESTA. I hear a voice…

MIKE. Forces my fingers to skate up the warm patch of panties and feel your heartbeat

VESTA. In the middle of all this swarming

MIKE. My hand against my will wedges under and gets tangled in the hairball of your sex

VESTA. Someone calling through the drone of all the bees

MIKE. And it's my bird finger that finally slides into you and I see your lower lip drop and your toes flex and your brow knits even deeper as deeper I go

VESTA. And I feel in my womb all the bees taking the shape of this light

MIKE. Then with you on my finger so golden warm and beautiful and the needle going up to 65, 70, 75, 80, 90, 98.6 –

VESTA. Are you her? Are you my mercy? Will all my cycles of men be for this tender loving grace?

MIKE. I feel her

VESTA. All my pains for you?

MIKE. I feel the soul of my girl, I

VESTA. Reach to kiss her, to kiss

MIKE. My baby girl, my

VESTA. Sweet deliverance, she is

MIKE. My poem
Part of that longer painer loner poem and suddenly

VESTA. My hand grips the door and flicks the power window and down it comes

MIKE. and her head just falls out in the deep fast nothing of the open road and

VESTA. my baby's kiss on my lips soars off into the night

MIKE/VESTA. like a silent luna moth

(She opens her mouth and the roar of wind and cars and time fill the room. Lights change. It's hella still.)

VESTA. I was pregnant.

(They turn again to the crib.)

MIKE. Oh shit.

VESTA. Sweet holy fuck.

(They slowly make their approach and peer in.)

We gotta find her, Mike.

MIKE. We will, I promise.

VESTA. This is our baby.

MIKE. We'll get her back right quick, I swear.

(They frantically search all over for the baby.)

VESTA. How? How??

Shit me! What've we done, Mike?

MIKE. We don't know that we done anything just yet. Think about it, Vesta. Would we hurt our own child? Could we really?

VESTA. We were shooting up.

MIKE. Yeah, okay. But besides that!

VESTA. How could we lose her, Mike! Our baby!

She came to me in a dream.

MIKE. Maybe she's still a dream. Maybe she's not real and we're bent out of shape for nothin'.

VESTA. Not real? Not real? Mike, I've been living my whole life dead. Living for the needs of others, walking a house with no room for me. I catch the clap the first time I have sex, and herpes on the next. Every time I try to love, Love guts me till I'm hardly even here. I'm a ghost. A womb full of hurt. My whole body this unbearable hole that I gotta fill with something, anything, booze, burgers, dope, cum, any goddamned thing. But finally I got something that really *fits.*

Something that'll love me back. She's real, holmes. Don't say she ain't or I will mess you up.

MIKE. You got herpes?

VESTA. I should mess you up, anyway.

MIKE. Awright, hold the shit up.

VESTA. She's real, Mike! SHE'S REAL!

MIKE. Okay! She's real! Then maybe…maybe we left her with somebody.

VESTA. Like who?

MIKE. Like, I dunno, friends, your parents!

VESTA. Not likely. I got a vague feeling that bridge got burned way back. Somethin' I did. Some really bad sin. I think I'm beyond redemption with them.

MIKE. Awright.

VESTA. What about your mom?

MIKE. What, my old lady? Are you kidding? She's the last person on earth I'd leave my kid with. Why would you even suggest that?

VESTA. I guess we both got bridges burned.

MIKE. Shit, babe, maybe *we are* ghosts and the kid's the only real one here.

VESTA. Maybe she's in the crib right now and we just can't see her.

MIKE. 'Cause we're ruined. Born ruined.

> (*Sudden violent banging on the door. Lights abruptly change.*)

ABEL. VERA! VERA!

VERA. Oh, god! It's Abel!

ABEL. I KNOW YOU'RE IN THERE!

MIKE. Holy shit!

ABEL. WOMAN OPEN UP! COME ON, VERA!

MIKE. Vera? I thought your name was…

VERA. Keep your voice down!

ABEL. VERA, I CAN HEAR YOU! I COME ALL THE WAY OUT HERE JUST TO SEE YOU. AND YOU KNOW HOW MUCH I HATE NEW MEXICO!

MIKE. New Mexico?

ABEL. THAT'S RIGHT. WHAT THE HELL POSSESSED Y'ALL TO MOVE TO TUCUMCARI?

VERA. Tucumcari?

ABEL. LET ME IN, BABY!!!

MIKE. *(toward the door)* Who is it?

ABEL. *(suddenly affable)* Hey, Mike. It's me, man. Open up.

MIKE. Am I supposed to know you?

VERA. Don't let him in.

MIKE. I don't think I know you.

ABEL. Aw hell, don't play games with me. I know you two got hitched.

VERA. We're married?

MIKE. It is my ring!

> *(They high-five.)*

ABEL. It's Abel! C'mon, just Abel, honey! I wanna talk!

MIKE. I don't wanna let him in.

VERA. Then don't let him in!

ABEL. *(in a sing-song voice)* I heard you got preggers!

> *(They freeze. The door opens itself. **ABEL** steps in, wearing his telephone gear belt like a gun holster.)*

I heard, anyway.

VERA. Well, you're mistaken. I'm not having no baby.

ABEL. Hey, Mike.

MIKE. Hey.

ABEL. You lookin' good.

MIKE. Thanks.

ABEL. Actually, you ain't lookin' all that good, now that I see you. You look awful pale and skinny. You hittin' that bottle again, boy?

MIKE. Yeah, but you know, it keeps hittin' back.

ABEL. I bet it do. Maybe you should put that in a poem. Heh. I heard you married my woman.

VERA. I'm not your woman, Abel.

ABEL. And I heard that you shot your semen in her. And that she's preggers.

VERA. Quit using that word. I hate that word.

MIKE. Where'd you hear all that?

ABEL. On the phone. I'm the telephone man. Yep. The word is out on you two.

VERA. Look, we just got married today. We been celebratin' the occasion.

ABEL. The whole blessed day?!
Vera, punkin, you shouldn't be drinkin' like that. It's not good for your health.

VERA. Since when'd you start caring so goddamn much about my goddamn health?

ABEL. Dang. How do you like the mouth on this cookie? Racy, ain't she?
Well, Vera, I always cared for your wellbeing. But I suppose I started caring more when you got yourself preggers.

MIKE. She's not preggers.

VERA. Pregnant!

ABEL. Oh, I beg to differ. Oh yes I do. I look at you, I place my hand right here on the little poochy part of your belly and I feel creation. I feel a million little cells fallin' into place and makin' life right in the pocket of your womanhood. I seen it on PBS. And since then, I have been amazed by the process of creation, how a little feeling in the pants can make a living breathing creature with the features of the father pasted right on its face. All the promise of this world curds into this devastatin' miracle we call a baby. Yeah, that little bitch is in there, all right. Aintcha?

> *(yelling into her womb)*

AINTCHA!!

MIKE. HEY!

VERA. Abel, you're hurting me!

MIKE. All right, all right, man! We're having a kid! There! Now you know. Now do you mind getting the fuck out so we can go on with our lives?

ABEL. Yes, I mind. 'Cause you don't know what she and I know. Right, Vera?

VERA. Abel, you're so fulla shit.

ABEL. We know, don't we?

MIKE. What's he talking about?

VERA. You got nothin' on me.

ABEL. We were meant to make babies, baby. Even before I knew you, Mama said, buy you a house, son. Pick a room and paint it pink and prep you for the comin' of life cause it's comin'! Then you came like a trucker's dream into my life. Dancing in your thong to "You Really Gotta Hold On Me." My beautiful bride. And didn't we try to conceive? Didn't we? Time after time, I do my level best to love a child into you, but nothing seems to work. I start to doubt the power of my Pecker Jones. I am a man diminished. Till Mama sees you at the pharmacy and whispers to me, find her wheel of fortune and get your manhood back. I search high and low till I find your pills taped under the bed. And I know my junk is potent and true, brimming with a legion of red-blooded little Abels ready to blow you up. I learn the power of a woman's lie is no match for me. I'm sorry that hell and doom rained on you for a while, and I'm sorry about your teeth, but you needed that poison pounded outa you. You are Vera the Woman of Abel and that Child is our Bond 'cause The Hootchie-Kootchie to End All Hootchie-Kootchie cannot be denied. I got a baby in you yet. UH! UH! UH!

MIKE. Is that true?

VERA. I'm not your Woman, I'm not your fool and my kid ain't no kind of bond.

You got no hold on me now.

ABEL. How do you figure?

VERA. 'Cause you had three jacks but I drew the ace of hearts. And won.

ABEL. Angel…

VERA. You listen to me, Abel.

I take my Vesta power and fuse it to Vera fury

and set right here at your feet a force-field of unimaginable juju

Which if you dare cross will burn your dick off and wither your nuts to paste!

YOU ARE NOTHING TO ME, AND NOTHING TO MY BABY, SO READ MY GLOSSY LIPS: YOU CROSS THAT LINE, THE ALMIGHTY WRATH OF ME IS GONNA FUCK YOU UP, MOTHERFUCKER!

MIKE. Damn.

Time you went, Abel. My wife and me got things to do.

ABEL. Do them. Do your things. Do them while you can. But remember this. You wed a woman in New Mexico that's still married in Texas, a woman who is carryin' her legal husband's child. When that child is born, I'll be back. Do things. Do your things.

MIKE. You won't find us. We're movin'.

VERA. I'm gonna be a teacher.

ABEL. You ever seen that old western movie, *The Searchers?* Think of me as John Wayne.

(He starts for the door. Stops.)

Do I smell chicken? Mm-mmm-mmm!

(He goes. The door closes. Lights change to the present.)

MIKE. How did he track us down? What is he, some kind of bounty hunter?

VERA. He's the Telephone Man.

MIKE. He called you Vera.

VERA. That must be my name.

MIKE. How come he knows it and I don't? And where did he get off claiming that it's his baby? How could he say that? What kind of craziness is that?

VERA. It ain't so crazy.

MIKE. You mean, he's right? It's his kid?

VERA. Mike.

MIKE. How far along were you? Back when you found out?

VERA. Along enough.

MIKE. So it could be his.

VERA. It's not.

MIKE. But it could. He came in here and said so. For all we know, he's the one who took the kid and left the drumstick just to rub it in our faces.

VERA. He's not the father, I'm telling you.

MIKE. There's a chance, though, right? Right?

VERA. Would it make any difference?

MIKE. Hell's bells, yes, it makes a difference! Whose kid am I raising?

VERA. So what you're saying is you don't want her.

MIKE. No! I mean –

VERA. That is what you're saying. You don't want to be this baby's daddy.

MIKE. That's not what I'm saying!

VERA. THEN WHAT THE FUCK ARE YOU SAYING, MIKE, CUZ SHE NEEDS TO KNOW WHERE YOU STAND!

MIKE. I DON'T FUCKEN KNOW!

(He crumbles into himself.)

daddy daddy what's daddy

I don't know what the word means just

another bittersweet nothing Mother used on all her johns hey

daddy come on in stay awhile daddy daddy you kind fly –

by-night daddies drinking out of my spiderman cup droppin'

ashes on my notebooks winkin'
at me on their way out see you
'round, daddy –

VERA. – Shit –

MIKE. they were honey bees and she the queen me
hardly even there most
times stayin' with my gramma most
times hidin' in my bed hidin' from my
constant dreams of washing my sins off
In a tub filled with the cum of all my daddies so
yah yah fuck the daddies and all the dots they leave
behind connect
the dots sweet Mother mine the little red dots swellin'
all over you
all. over. you.

    (a long breath)

VERA. Mike. The baby's yours. You wanna have a test, we'll
have a test.

    (**MIKE** *looks at* **VERA** *for a spell.*)

MIKE. Baby, we don't need a test. This life is a test. I need
something to believe in. You say she's mine, that's good
enough for me.

VERA. Connect the dots. Little red dots. It's a road map.

MIKE. Road map?

VERA. Between us and Abel, your old lady and all that
fucken shit.

MIKE. Where the rubbers meet the road.

    (Lights change.)

VERA. We hit the road

MIKE. Our Falcon on the wing

VERA. With precious cargo

MIKE. West to somewhere

VERA. Further out than ever

MIKE. Where they won't get to us

VERA. Past grain silos

MIKE. And water towers

VERA. Past a painted desert

MIKE. A forest of petrified trees

VERA. A big-ass crater in the middle of somewhere

MIKE. Feeling the new wind in our faces

VERA. And the pull of old obligations

MIKE. Till we're standing on a corner

VERA. In Winslow Ariz –

Hold up.

> (**VERA** *feels the surface of the table.*)

There's something here.

MIKE. In Winslow, Arizona

VERA. I know it. I remember.

MIKE. On a day when you've been gone all day and the day's all gone too

> (*She reaches under the table and peels off a small photograph.*)

What's that?

> (*Lights change.*)

What's going on, Vera? What you got there?

VERA. I went to the baby doctor today.

MIKE. You did? Wasn't the appointment for next week?

VERA. Yeah, but I went today.

MIKE. Why didn't you tell me? I was supposed to go.

VERA. Well, to be honest, I was scared that all our boozin' an' shit had messed with our baby. So I went in and got me an ultrasound to be sure. I didn't know what I'd see. I thought if there was something wrong with her, I might, you know…

MIKE. What?

VERA. Take care of it.

MIKE. Fuck.

What've you done, Vera? What've you done to our baby?

VERA. It was so easy…

MIKE. Oh no…no…

VERA. I just had to say the word.

MIKE. Tell me you didn't, Vera. You didn't.

(She offers the photograph to **MIKE.***)*

VERA. I didn't. She's all right.

MIKE. She? Did you say she?

Oh my god. She's beautiful.

VERA. I almost did it, Mike. I almost lost her.

It's no big deal.

The whole family planning thing. I done it before.

When I was fifteen, I got knocked up.

Fucker swore to Jesus it wasn't his, but I knew better. So I did it.

I went in there by myself. Not him, not my mom, not even Jesus.

Just me.

MIKE. What about your dad?

VERA. He told me to go.

MIKE. I thought he was a Man of God.

VERA. Oh, he was.

MIKE. Did he kick your boyfriend's ass?

VERA. He woulda.

If he weren't the boyfriend too.

*(***MIKE** *is speechless.)*

Did I just say that?

MIKE. Shit, babe.

VERA. I did, didn't I? Wow.

That day was strange.

I lost two things I hated and wanted very badly.

A father and a son.

We *are* ruined people, Mike.

MIKE. Not this time, babe.
You and me, we both got shit in the loss column.
But now we're doin' it right. It's meant to be.
Check it out.

> *(the ultrasound photo)*

This is divinity.

VERA. She looks like she's in mid-cartwheel.

MIKE. Hell, she's dancin'. Baby's doin' the limbo. The
pony. The two-step. The cumbia!
We got us a dancin' fool, honey! Aaaoooh!

> *(He dances around with the photo.)*

This girl is gonna set the world on fire with her moves!
You watch! She will!
We're not losing her, Vera.
If we do, they win.

VERA. Straight up?

MIKE. Straight way up.

VERA. Then we gotta change, holmes. We gotta quit
partyin' if we're serious about her.
We gotta start acting like parents or we're gonna lose
this tiny dancer.

MIKE. What are you sayin'? No more Dewar's?

VERA. No more Dewar's.

MIKE. Fuck it. Let's do it. Stone cold turkey. Just pour that
shit out and be done with it.
We live for her now.

> *(He takes one long draw from the bottle.)*

Starting now.

VERA. You hear that, little punk?
You gonna be our indie girl, all the way!

> *(The lights change to the present. VERA collapses
> into tears.)*

(sobbing uncontrollably) Oh my god. Jesus God.

MIKE. Easy, babe. C'mon. I'm here. I'm right here.

VERA. My own daddy, Mike! Fuck!

MIKE. Maybe that part wasn't real. Maybe it's only in your head.

VERA. It has to be real. It hurts too much not to be.
Yeah. Yeah. I remember. The dead of night. Him slipping in my sheets.
Moving inch by inch into the Kingdom of Heaven, kissin'
scripture in my ear the whole time.
"Oh dove, oh undefiled."
The real Song of Songs, the real-real of me.

MIKE. I'll tell you what. Real to me is your voice on the phone that very first night. Real to me is dreaming the same baby together. Real is this, right here, right now.

VERA. Mike. I wanted it. It was God's love.

MIKE. That ain't no kind of love. And you musta known it, messed up as you were,
You musta known it.

VERA. Now that you know…does it matter, Mike? Do you still want me?

MIKE. I want you more.

> (*They kiss. The ultrasound photo.* **VERA** *scrutinizes the image. Then she turns it around.*)

VERA. Whoa. How did we miss this?

MIKE. What?

VERA. There's writing on the back.

> (*reading*)

Your death's-head angel
Caught in the womblight
Of the ultrasound
Miguel, Miguel.
Your destiny curled in
my lucent *huesos.*

Is this your handwriting?

MIKE. I think so.

> (**VERA** *takes the photo.*)

VERA. It's not a bad poem.

MIKE. It's not a poem yet. Just the fetus of a poem.

VERA. What does *huesos* mean?

MIKE. Bones.

VERA. Your destiny curled in
my lucent *bones.*
It's like the kid is talking to you.
In Spanish

MIKE. Too bad. 'Cause all I mainly know is the cuss words.

VERA. Me too.

MIKE. *Cabrona.*

VERA. *Pendejo.*

MIKE. *Chinga tu madre.*

VERA. *Hijo de puta.*

MIKE. *¡Caca mushy de gato blanco en la boca, guey!*

VERA. *¡Culo de caballo viejo con las runs, guey!*

> (*They laugh.*)

Hold the phone. It called you "Miguel."
It's says you're not a Mike. You're a Miguel.

MIGUEL. My third grade teacher called me Migwell. She used to say "Migwell, go to the board. Migwell, you have an uncommon way with words." I thought she meant I couldn't spell. But then one day she said "Migwell, you should write a poem."

VERA. Is that what you do? Are you trying to be some kinda poet?

MIGUEL. That explains why we're poor.

VERA. Don't be a wiseass. You wanna be a poet. Our kid in the ultrasound is saying your destiny is in its bones. Miguel the poet has to finish the fetus of this poem to make our baby real.

MIGUEL. You know how crazy you sound right now?

VERA. Oh my god. These poems. Before, you couldn't read them 'cause you were Mike. But now you're Miguel!

> (**VERA** *rushes to the floor and collects the balled up wads of paper.* **MIKE** *scans over them.*)

Well? You wrote them, didn't you?

MIGUEL. They're my shitty poems, all right.
Poems of living with my *abuela* in her *casita,*
riding my banana seat bike to *la tienda,*
eating *chili verde* with Mexican Coca-Cola,
the beat-down life *de mi gente,*

VERA. They don't sound so shitty to me.

MIGUEL. Poems about a little punk-ass kid holed up in his room putting down words while he listens for his Ama's raggedy *voz* through the door. *Abuela* sayin' don't wait up for her. All of them don't-wait-up poems. *Odas* for a Woman named Cristina.

VERA. Cristina.

MIGUEL. A Woman I call Ama
But the good-time *Fulanos* call Cristina.
Se llama Cristina is the title.
All of them titled *Se Llama Cristina.*

I get to college…fuck, it was a writing scholarship too. In my class, these words forming, *palabras negras* I can't bring myself to put down. Demon verses *en el idioma de mi casa* drifting from English to Spanish like undocumented memories of Cristina. So I walk away. I drop out and walk away from it all. Me and my big butt-ugly Cristina poems filling *mis huesos* even my fucken dreams
with this unnameable want.

VERA. Okay.
Name it.

> (*He preps himself. Poised over paper. Struggles.*)

Do it, *Miguel.*

MIGUEL. I can't.

VERA. For the baby, holmes.

MIGUEL. *¡No puedo!*

VERA. Migwell! Go to the board!

MIGUEL. No! I'm not doin' it. I don't got the words. They don't come to me anymore, they don't wanna come.

VERA. Then you gotta go to them. I know you can do it!

MIGUEL. Those words are nothin'. Notes. Doodles. Abortions. No way no way no way.

> (**MIGUEL** *gets up and goes for the bottle of Dewar's.*)

VERA. Hey, what the fuck. We made a deal.

MIGUEL. You made a deal.

VERA. No, Miguel.

MIGUEL. Let me go!

> (**VERA** *yanks the Dewar's away.*)

VERA. WHAT'S THE MATTER WITH YOU? WE PROMISED, MIGUEL! FOR OUR KID, DAMMIT! WE GOTTA HOLD ON! WE GOTTA MAKE SURE WE DON'T FORGET THE THINGS THAT COUNT! EVEN IF IT KILLS US!

MIGUEL. IT **IS** KILLIN' US!

> (*They wrestle for the bottle. Suddenly she doubles over in pain. Lights change.*)

VERA. Oh! Jeez!

MIGUEL. What.

VERA. Holy mother.

MIGUEL. Is it time?

VERA. Hold on.

MIGUEL. Do we go now?

VERA. Hold the fuck up, babe.

MIGUEL. I can get us there in seven minutes flat. Five if I get all the greens. Winslow's dead at this hour!

VERA. Shut up a minute and let me think.

MIGUEL. Okay.

VERA. No. No. The doctor said women tend to show up too early, they got no threshold for pain. But I do, and I feel not too dilated right now.

MIGUEL. Really.

VERA. Not that dilated. Two, three centimeters max.

MIGUEL. So you don't wanna go.

VERA. Hell no. I'm cool. I'm chill.

(pain)

Holy Mother!

MIGUEL. ¿*Que pasó?*

VERA. Put the TV on.

MIGUEL. *Bueno,* where's the remote?

VERA. Right there.

MIGUEL. Cool. Where's the TV?

VERA. Right there.

MIGUEL. Awesome.

(He turns on the TV.)

Nomas give me the word, and I'll get the car.

VERA. When I hit five centimeters we go.

(They stare at the TV for a moment, tensely.)

I'm terrified, Miguel.

What if she's like us?

MIGUEL. She is us.

VERA. No, I'm saying what if she turns out to be a fuckup *just like us?*

If everything's bad, how can she possibly turn out good?

MIGUEL. She has to be good. That's what I keep telling myself. The problem ain't her. It's us. What if we're worse than our parents? What if we take all the *mierda* they gave us out on her? She doesn't deserve that, does she?

I could use a fifth of courage.

VERA. I'm thinking the same thing, holmes. It's been months.

MIKE. Don't we keep a fifth somewhere?

(**MIGUEL** *finds it.* **VERA** *slugs one down.*)

VERA. Lord, I needed that.

Hey, is that John Wayne?

MIGUEL. Oh. Shit. You know what this is? *The Searchers.*

(**ABEL**'s *voice.*)

ABEL. It's kinda funny, huh?

(**ABEL** *enters from out of nowhere.*)

How we measure the coming of life. Funny as hell.

VERA. motherfucker.

ABEL. Remarkable how the dilation of that sweet hole of pleasure is the measure of new life. Coming not in miles, nor feet, nor pints, but centimeters. When did we get on the metric system in this country, anyways?

MIGUEL. How the fuck did you get in?

ABEL. You got the crib too. Judging from the color, I expect a little cowgirl to make her debut.

MIGUEL. Get the hell out of my house! Now!

ABEL. Easy, Pancho. Vera knows she just has to think of me and here I be.

VERA. I wasn't thinking of you.

ABEL. Oh, I beg to differ. Oh yes I do. I know exactly the context you were thinking me into. You were thinkin' what if this encumbrance is better off with Abel.

VERA. I wasn't thinking that. Plus my kid is not an encumbrance.

MIGUEL. *Mira, cabrón.* I'm not telling you twice! Get away from my wife!

VERA. Get the overnight bag, Miguel.

ABEL. You're not gonna make it. That old Ford Falcon you got? It's gotta flat.

(**MIGUEL** *rushes to the window and looks out.*)

MIGUEL. *¡Chinga la madre!*

VERA. *¡Hijo de puta!*

ABEL. How's the dilation now, honey?

MIGUEL. All right! I've had it with you!

>(**MIGUEL** *rushes* **ABEL** *who subdues him with a single move.* **MIGUEL** *lands on the floor with a thud.*)

VERA. ABEL! LEAVE HIM ALONE!

>(**ABEL** *pours the Dewar's on her lap.*)

Ow! What the fuck!

ABEL. Lookit. Your dam just broke. You musta jumped from five to ten centimeters in the space of a breath. I'm not surprised. There's a full moon out, a big ol' thunder moon at that, and that means the tidal push and pull of all the waters on this side of the planet kinda heave creation forward some. You feel her?

>(**VERA** *winces.* **MIGUEL** *winces.* **ABEL** *turns to mess with the phone.*)

I told you. Didn't I? I'm back for her.

MIGUEL. Vera. Vera. You okay?

VERA. I have to go to the hospital.

MIGUEL. I know but this turd punctured our –

VERA. I have to go. RIGHT NOW!

MIGUEL. I'm callin' 911.

ABEL. That's why I'm here. There's been some service disruptions in this area code and I been assigned to repair the lines. I tell you, it's not lookin' good…

>(**ABEL** *tosses the phone to* **MIGUEL**. *Tries to dial. No dial tone.*)

MIGUEL. FUCK! What've you done, *ese?*

VERA. Oh god, Miguel…!

ABEL. Phone lines are gonna be dead for a while. It's a good thing you called me when you did.

MIGUEL. What the hell are you talking about?

ABEL. You don't know? She called me, Mike.

VERA. No, no! I didn't!

ABEL. C'mon, Vera, tell the truth for once.

MIGUEL. You called him?

VERA. Okay, I called him. While you were looking for work. But he didn't answer and I hung up.

ABEL. She left a message, though.

MIGUEL. What!

VERA. I did not leave a message! Abel, you are such a liar! I didn't leave him any such message, not a word! You have to believe that.

ABEL. No, you stay on the line and say nothing, you say nothing at all which speaks volumes. I'm standing there by the answering machine, wondering if it's you or some ghost of you. Then I hear through the white hiss of the line: a sigh. You sigh into my machine and hang up.

MIGUEL. You sighed?

ABEL. *(sighing once piteously)* Just like that.
Now what's it mean, Vera? This sigh dropped on your husband's ear five hunnerd sixty one point nine miles away on the day you are to deliver our baby?
What does it mean?

VERA. It's not *your* baby.

MIGUEL. What does that sigh mean, Vera? Why did you call him and leave him a sigh?

VERA. Now is not the time to ask this shit.

MIGUEL. Why did you leave him a sigh?

VERA. 'Cause I'm scared! I'm scared, Miguel, that we're not going to make it. I'm scared that my baby's gonna end up like me! Damaged goods, a loser birthing one more loss, one more failer in this world. *(pain)* Ow! What do you want with a sideshow like me? All my dreams are small-town dreams. All my stories end with I told you so. I know I'll never get a teaching interview. But you still gotta chance! Go back to school, write your ass off, write those beat-down poems and don't let me drag you down. *(pain)*

ABEL. Pack your bags, Migwell. You can still catch the last hound at the station.

VERA. Jesus!

ABEL. Lie back, baby. Abel's here now.

> (**MIGUEL** *rushes to the couch, and from deep in the cushions produces a bottle of dewar's. He sucks down a draw of whiskey.*)

VERA. Holy mother!

ABEL. *(peeking in her dress)* Oh babe. Too late for Winslow Memorial, I'd say.

VERA. Mike.

> (**MIGUEL** *heads for the door. It opens. He can see his freedom.*)

ABEL. He's gone. He's running down the stairs. Chasing down the good life somewhere not here

VERA. Miguel

ABEL. He's kickin' the Falcon's tire and walkin' the lonesome streets of Winslow

VERA. Wait

ABEL. There's a spring in his step as he breathes in the freein' desert air

VERA. Don't fuckin' leave me like this

ABEL. And he buys himself a ticket back to Canyon and boards the wheezin' graveyard bus.

> (**MIGUEL** *takes a step out and disappears from view.* **ABEL** *kneels before* **VERA** *and places her feet on his shoulders as he prepares to deliver the baby.*)

I can see her now. She's crowning. Crowning out to her Daddy's hands

VERA. Oh baby girl, you my *Mujer Libre,* hold on hold on tight to me

ABEL. Oh I see her dark and pinched and bloody

VERA. You don't want this man to be your father

ABEL. so ready to cry piss eat fuck and die
     as the spawn of a telephone man

VERA. Hold tight to me *and call out the name of your true
     daddy!*

ABEL. In the recurring tale of Abel and Vera
     a girl is born and named after my sweet Momma!
     Gimme! Gimme! Gimme! Gimme!

>   (**VERA** *shrieks the name of her* **MAN** *with the power
>   of two voices.*)

VERA. Miguel!

>   (**MIGUEL** *abruptly returns and pushes* **ABEL**
>   *away.*)

MIGUEL. No.
     That's not how it is. That's not how it is!
     Yeah I gotta flat, yeah the phones go dead all over
     Winslow, yeah the kid starts coming fast. But I am here.
     I'm here for all of it! Right, baby? Right?

VERA. Damn straight.

MIGUEL. We deliver our baby girl in this crummy apartment
     and I cut the umbilical cord with a steak knife. But I
     stay! That's how it happens in *my* poem!

>   (**ABEL** *walks* **MIGUEL** *right up against the wall.
>   The dial tone on the phone suddenly comes on.*)

Looks like the lines are up again, big guy.

ABEL. I'll get her. When you least expect me,
     I'll slip into her life and bedazzle her with my brawn
     and song and take her away.
     And you won't be able to do a goddamn thing about it.

One way or another.

>   (*He goes. The phone continues its tone.* **MIGUEL**
>   *and* **VERA** *look at each other, then* **MIGUEL** *slowly
>   goes to the phone. He picks up the receiver. Lights
>   change.*)

MIGUEL. *¿Bueno? ¿Ama? ¿Eres tu? Soy yo. Miki. Espérate. No digas nada. Quiero que me escuches.*
Toda mi vida me he sentido como un huérfano. Como estranjero en mi país, mi casa, mi cuerpo. Asi he pasado mi vida. Pero yo sé que salí de tu vientre, y tu nombre es mi nombre, en mi cara tus ojos lloran, en mis venas corre tu sangre. No estoy solo. Caminas conmigo, tu alma empañada con la mía. Eso lo acabo de notar. Y ahora quiero decirte que tú tampoco no caminas sola. Tienes una nieta, Ama. Mi esposa dio luz. At three this morning. A darling little girl. *Este milagro va alumbrar a nuestro mundo. Quiero que sepas, Ama.*

(He puts the phone down. Lights change.)

VERA. Damn, who the fuck are you?

MIKI. Miki. That was her baby-name for me.

VERA. How you feeling.

MIKI. Kinda…

VERA. Me too.

MIKI. That call, all I could hear on the other line was cryin'. Never said a word.

VERA. Wouldna been proper.

MIKI. I remember now. How she tried. She really tried to do her best. She just wasn't cut out for it. You know, you look like Ama. In her more sober moments.

VERA. That's why you never dated Mexicans.

MIKI. And why I fell head over toenails for you.

VERA. We pulled off a miracle, Miki. Un milagro.

MIKI. I remember holding this tiny little thing in my hands. Feeling so helpless.

VERA. She was.

MIKI. I wasn't talking about the baby.

(They go to the crib.)

VERA. M.I.A.

MIKI. What's her name?

VERA. Baby doesn't have a name. I want to name her Marie after my sister, but you won't let me.

MIKI. Marie just doesn't sound right.

> (**VERA** *takes the chicken leg from the crib and holds
> it like a baby.*)

VERA. Kid. Kid is what we call you.
I look at your sweet guileless face,
them big brown Mexican eyes, and I can tell,
Oh, you are gonna kick my ass,
'Cause that's what babies do.
They keep it real.
You keep me real.
Can I tell you a secret?
I'm never gonna be a teacher.
I thought I'd be a really good teacher
But I been kidding myself the whole time.
So you are what I'm pinning my dreams on,
My song of songs.
"the only one of her mother.
the only choice" of my life.

MIKI. You know you're talkin' to a leg of chicken, right?

VERA. Now it comes back to me. We move!

MIKI. Again?

VERA. Right after she's born

MIKI. Where

VERA. As far west as she goes

MIKI. And that means

MIKI/VERA. California!!!

VERA. Golden hills!

MIKI. Golden prospects!

VERA. San Francisco!

MIKI. Nope. Daly City

VERA. Daly City? Daly fucken City? Why?

MIKI. It's all we can afford

VERA. Oh yeah

MIKI. Right on the edge of the fog belt. With the ocean just
out of view

VERA. All just enough to make us feel smaller than we ever
have

MIKI. If that's possible

VERA. But we do it for you

MIKI. They got poetry workshops everywhere

VERA. I stay home, breast-feedin' the loudest kid in the
Trade Winds Motel

MIKI. While I get work at the Home Depot moving crates
and boxes

VERA. And you break your thumb

MIKI. FUUUCK!

> *(Lights change.)*

> *(The loud persistent crying of the baby fills the
space.)*

> *(**MIKI** and **VERA** are riding the razor edge of
sobriety.)*

VERA. Now look what you did. You woke the baby.
I finally get her quiet and you crow like a idiot and wake
her!

MIKI. I'm disabled, Vera! Disabled!

VERA. Stupid job at stupid Home Depot! You can't even do
that without busting your damn thumb!

MIKI. *Ya no lo aguanto.*

> *(**MIKI** makes for the door.)*

VERA. Where do you think you're going?

MIKI. Out.

VERA. You can't be serious, holmes. I got dinner ready.

MIKI. I need some air.

VERA. You supposed to be writing, Miki.

MIKI. How can I do anything with the kid crying and crying
all the – arrggg! I could use a break.

VERA. And I could use some help. I got a colicky baby and food on the stove, dumbass!

MIKI. How am I gonna help with this?

VERA. Well, then, do something useful. Like give our baby a name.

MIKI. What's the rush?

VERA. What's the rush? She needs to know her name! We can't call her "kid" forever.

MIKI. Kid sounds fine to me. I'll see you.

VERA. Uh-uh. You ain't goin' nowhere.

MIKI. Get the fuck outa the way, Vera.

VERA. We need you to stay home!

MIKI. Home? This ain't no home. This is squalor. This is a dead end. This ain't my California Dream!

VERA. Oh, is that what you want? I'm busting my ass in our roach motel raising the kid with next to nothin' and you want to dream?

MIKI. Please make that kid stop. For the love of God!

VERA. Take a marijuana minute and think about this, you sick drunk Jerry Springer butthole loser. I got no time for dreams. I'm too busy staying up all hours of the night with this kid and making your damn chicken dinner, asshole!

MIKI. Don't bust your ass on my account.

VERA. Then you know what? You know what? The chicken is not for you. It is for the kid!

(**VERA** drops the chicken leg in the crib.)

MIKI. Great! Just great! See ya!!

VERA. No way! Not till you name our baby!

MIKI. *¡Como jodes!*

VERA. I don't get it. What's wrong with giving our baby a name? Why won't you name her?

MIKI. Don't you see? Naming it makes it real! Naming the kid dooms her!

VERA. You think our baby's doomed?

MIKI. We're all doomed! Look around! Things are no better! They're worse! We're not parents. I'm not a writer and you're not a teacher. And she's not…she's not ever gonna…

Open your eyes, Vera. It's over! We're done!

We should just go home to Texas and hope it still wants us back.

VERA. You know what you are? A wrong number.

I dialed the wrong number and got stuck with you.

MIKI. And I got stuck with a used-up rodeo stripper whore!

VERA. Here's a newsflash! She ain't your kid!

You can't name her 'cause she ain't your kid!

MIKI. Then whose is it? Your Daddy, maybe? "O Love, O undefiled!"

> (**VERA** *slaps him. He takes her face in his hands and roars all the bile of his life into it. She breaks away and smashes directly into the table, which strikes her square in the face. The baby's cries abruptly stop.* **VERA** *holds her mouth with both hands and then spits out a single tooth. Then spits out another. Then another. And finally one more. They look at each other. Horrified,* **MIKI** *swings open the door and crosses the threshold, but then turns around again. At the same time,* **VERA** *rushes to the bathroom but stops at the doorway. Each of them suspended on the threshold of some new desperation.*)

I rush out and down the stairs and slam-dance into the parking lot

VERA. I wash my mouth out screaming at that bitch in the bathroom mirror

MIKI. Stomping at that ugly shadow at my feet

VERA. The baby finally calm in the wake of my sobs

MIKI. Headin' to the bar with the broken neon

VERA. Goin' to the crib and lookin' through my tears

MIKI. Wantin' to put somethin' in my mouth that hurts

VERA. I wanna nurse you, baby, but my tits are so damned sore

MIKI. But I can't bring myself to swallow

VERA. All my secret Dewar's going down like vinegar

MIKI. OH FUCKIN' JESUS

VERA. SHIT

MIKI. How do we unruin this

VERA. I wanna cry uncle. I wanna take it all back

MIKI. I head out to the freeway like maybe I'll get lucky and get pancaked by a semi

VERA. Head-first into the closet and rip up his favorite shirts

which is only two

and one of them is mine

MIKI. but there under the interstate I see a girl of sixteen or so and she's lookin' this way

VERA. And I realize I still got the teeth in my hand and I hear a faraway voice

MIKI. And the little tweaker offers me a bag and says

VERA. Take it, *ese*

MIKI. Her eyes the color of lemon peel and she says

VERA. When it gets really really bad, *ese*, and you just wanna take five, take this

MIKI. I hand her a Jackson and she disappears into a cardboard box up under where the pigeons roost

VERA. And the next thing I know, he's back.

     (turning to him)

Where are we *now?*

MIKI. What does it matter?

Wherever we go, we end up in the same rathole,

running smack into ourselves every time –

I bought us a little vacation.

     (MIKI *pours from the bag the works for shooting up.)*

VERA. Holy mother.

What's the catch?

MIKI. The catch is there is no catch.

VERA. Rack 'em up.

> (**MIKI** *and* **VERA** *sit across from each other at the table.* **MIKI** *gets the works out. he takes the little packet out and pours the powder onto the spoon.*)

Wait. What about the kid?

MIKI. The kid?

VERA. Our kid.

MIKI. Right now, Vera, there's only you and me. Only you and me matter.

VERA. She's not here?

MIKI. Not right now.

VERA. She's a third wheel.

MIKI. A weight.

VERA. An encumbrance, he said.

MIKI. Yeah. Encumbrance.

VERA. So. What we're saying is. There is no kid. There is absolutely no kid.

MIKI. What. Kid.

> (**MIKI** *and* **VERA** *look toward the crib. then look at each other.*)

> (*This is the crux of their crime.*)

> (**VERA** *holds up the spoon with the shit.* **MIKI** *takes the lighter and flicks it. When the flame comes on, everything turns to night. All the lights are out. A* **GIRL** *appears at the window, peering in. She quietly opens it and crawls in.* **MIKI** *and* **VERA** *watch her.*)

GIRL. ¿*Que pasó?*

You guys got any gum?

I know what you're thinking.

Don't trip.

GIRL. *(cont.)* It's better this way.
Like a thief in the night.
Come in thro *la ventana* like moonshine.
Without a sound.
Like love.
Far as you concerned, I ain't here.

    (The lighter goes out.)

So if anyone asks, you know what I mean?
I'm just a rumor, somethin' you heard about that mighta come true. Or not.
Yo, why's it so dark in here?

    (She turns on a light.)

What you doin'?
Oh, *vatos.*
That's the devil's drip.
You musta hit a low point.
You musta need to kill off a little soul.
Todas las pendejadas, todos los dolores, all your ragged miles come to this.
Heavy shit.

    (She laughs.)

Hey can you do this?

    (She executes a perfect cartwheel.)

I learned it in Acrosports camp when I was a *mocosa.* My dad took me to San Fran every weekend *en los veranos y aprendí* somersaults, backspins, twirls, all kinds of rope acrobatics. Let me tell you, the stuff comes in handy when you're trying to leap out of a moving car.

Hey, check this out!

    (She performs a pirouette and a jeté.)

Tight, huh? My moms taught me that one. She's a dance teacher and I sit in on her classes sometimes. Whenever this Indie girl needs to shake off the stress, *sabes?* Shake off the so-called man too. *Mujer Libre* all the way, that's me…

    (She sees the ultrasound photo.)

Aw, fresh. Is this your kid? Is this what's driving you to smack? Must be a girl, huh?

    *(***VERA*** *looks toward the crib and the* ***GIRL*** *turns and sees it for the first time.)*

Aw.

Look.

Qué linda.

What's your name.

You look like somebody I know.

In the eyes.

Dead ringer.

Sweet thing.

Life has some real surprises for you.

Ah, you gonna dig it.

Shh. Shh.

Baby gotta sleep.

Shh.

Little thing.

    (She steps away and throws herself on the couch.)

Thass a super-duper cutie you got.

I was a colicky little fuck testing my moms and pops every inch of the way.

Making all this mad crazy racket just to see them cope.

But I got better. It gets better.

    (She suddenly leaps to her feet.)

Oh man. I got the roamies. Don't you feel that, the roamies sending this crazy buzz into my body, I feel it and I gotta go gotta go gotta go don't matter where or how just hit the highway hitch across the desert to nowhere for no reason why, this buzz don't you feel it? like a drone in the bones making you roam, I was in the inconvenience store getting a microwave burrito when POW like a taser the roamies hit and I knew I had to go *sola* like a *chola* thumblin' through the torrid zones but he didn't like it, he was rough and mean and I broke it off for good, ooh that buzz like a thousand bees and me the hive! –

(**ABE**'s *voice roars outside the door. Everyone jolts.*)

ABE. KID!

GIRL. Oh god!

(**MIKI** *and* **VERA** *flinch at the pounding on the door.*)

ABE. KID, I KNOW YOU'RE IN THERE! I COME FOR YOU! OPEN UP!

GIRL. *(trying to cover her terror)* I got this. I got this. Don't say a word.

(*shouting, to* **ABE**)

Abe! Why don't you get fucked, *baboso!*

ABE. IT'S TIME YOU COME HOME WITH ME!

GIRL. NO *PINCHI* WAY!

ABE. AM I GONNA HAVE TO BUST DOWN THIS DOOR?

GIRL. YOU TRY IT, DUMBASS!

ABE. I WILL! I SWEAR!

GIRL. WELL, COME ON, BIG TALKER!

(*A horrible extended roar on the other side of the door.*)

ABE. RRRRRRRRRROOOOOOOOOWWWWWWWRRRRR GGGGGGG!

(*Then a loud thud against the door.*)

Ow.

GIRL. Abe? Are you there?

ABE. I'm hurt, honey. Open the door.

GIRL. No way.

ABE. C'mon. I love you. I even wrote a song for you.

GIRL. You did?

ABE. Right from the heart. You wanna hear it?

GIRL. *Pos…*

ABE. Lissen.

(He sings a bad song rather beautifully.)

BEHOLD, YOU ARE BEAUTIFUL, MY DOVE.
YOU BRING ALL GOOD THINGS TO ME.
YOU ARE THE WATER ON MY LIPS.
YOU ARE THE WARMTH ON MY BED.
YOU MAKE MY GARDEN GROW.
YOU MAKE MY AUTO GO.

*(The door opens and **ABE** steps in singing. **VERA** cringes when she sees him. **MIKI** clenches his fists. But they remain locked where they are.)*

I AM A BAD MAN IN MY WORLD
BUT I'M A GOOD MAN IN YOURS.
YOUR ROCK-STEADY LOVE SAVES ME DAILY.
DON'T LEAVE ME, BABY.
DON'T GO.
DON'T LEAVE ME, HONEY.
DON'T GO.
DON'T GO.
WOH-OH-OH.

So what it is now? You done with me?

GIRL. Hell yes.

ABE. Just like that.

GIRL. Just like that.

ABE. Look, I know we had problems, but everyone has problems.

GIRL. Your problems almost separated my shoulder.

ABE. I was rough, I admit it. But you just bring it out in a guy sometimes.

GIRL. So it's my fault?

ABE. No. It's my fault and I'm sorry. But you're rough too, you know. My junk is still sore.

GIRL. Well. I'm sorry about that.

ABE. I know I'm beneath you. I know there's no future in me. You're more than I hope to deserve.

GIRL. Then why do you even try?

ABE. 'Cause I deserve to hope.

Look, baby, you're done roamin'. Let's just quit this and go home. I'll make you some lasagna.

You like lasagna, don't you?

GIRL. I love lasagna.

ABE. Then whattaya say?

It's all gonna change now. I'm a new man.

GIRL. You won't change, Abe.

ABE. Oh, I beg to differ. Oh yes I do.

You know what you want; you just don't see it.

Come on out to the car, baby.

We'll party.

> *(**ABE** offers her a stick of gum.)*

Gum?

GIRL. Damn, Abe. How do you do it?

> *(He smirks. She takes it.)*

ABE. Who're these losers?

GIRL. Witnesses.

Go wait downstairs.

ABE. *(to **MIKI** and **VERA**)* See? One way or another.

> *(He goes.)*

GIRL. *Bueno, mi locos.* Thanks for the little courtesies. I hope that shit gives you the peace you're lookin' for.

> *(The **GIRL** takes the ultrasound photo and reads the poem in the back.)*

Death's-head angel. I like that.

> *(She peels off a piece of her gum and sticks it onto the ultrasound photo and plants it right over his heart. She starts to go after **ABE**. Stops. Turns.)*

He ain't so bad.

GIRL. Is he?

> (**VERA** *takes up the spoon while* **MIKE** *takes up the lighter. He flicks on the flame and they lock on it for a moment.* **VERA** *drops the spoon,* **MIKI** *turns off the flame. And sweeps the whole works off the table. The* **GIRL** *slams and locks the door.*)

What was I thinkin'. I can't go with him. I never liked his lasagna, anyways. I gotta roam.

> (*The* **GIRL** *grabs the chicken leg, latching her teeth onto it, and starts to slip out the window.*)

> (*She turns to* **MIKI** *and* **VERA** *one last time.*)

Ay los watcho.

> (*She vanishes into the night. Lights change.* **MIKI** *and* **VERA** *hold hands across the table. Well, almost. Then they hear the sweet gurgling sound of their baby.* **VERA** *wipes her face and scrambles to the crib and stands looking in for a long time. She reaches in and lifts her sleeping baby out and holds her close.* **MIKI** *nods.*)

MIKI. Cristina.

> (**VERA** *looks at* **MIKI**.)

VERA. Cristina Marie.

> (**MIKI** *takes a sheet of paper from the floor and a pencil nub and waits. Poised to begin. Blackout.*)

End of Play

www.ingramcontent.com/pod-product-compliance
Lightning Source LLC
Chambersburg PA
CBHW070418120726
47909CB00005B/1702